PENELOPE LIVELY

A LONG NIGHT AT
ABU SIMBEL

PENGUIN BOOKS

PENGUIN BOOKS

Published by the Penguin Group. Penguin Books Ltd, 27 Wrights Lane,
London w8 5tz, England. Penguin Books USA Inc., 375 Hudson Street,
New York, New York 10014, USA. Penguin Books Australia Ltd, Ringwood,
Victoria, Australia. Penguin Books Canada Ltd, 10 Alcorn Avenue, Toronto,
Ontario, Canada m4v 3b2. Penguin Books (NZ) Ltd, 182–190 Wairau Road,
Auckland 10, New Zealand · Penguin Books Ltd, Registered Offices: Har-
mondsworth, Middlesex, England · **These stories are taken from *Pack of
Cards* by Penelope Lively, published by Penguin Books in 1987.** This edition
published 1995 · Copyright © Penelope Lively, 1978, 1980, 1981, 1982, 1984,
1985, 1986. All rights reserved · The moral right of the author has been asserted ·
Typeset by Datix International Limited, Bungay, Suffolk. Printed in England by
Clays Ltd, St Ives plc · Except in the United States of America, this book is sold
subject to the condition that it shall not, by way of trade or otherwise, be lent, Har-
sold, hired out, or otherwise circulated without the publisher's prior consent in any
form of binding or cover other than that in which it is published and without a
similar condition including this condition being imposed on the subsequent pur-
chaser · 10 9 8 7 6 5 4 3 2 1

CONTENTS

A Long Night at Abu Simbel

In Cairo they had complained about the traffic and at Saqqara Mrs Marriott-Smith and Lady Hacking had wanted a lavatory and blamed her when eventually they had to retire, bleating, behind a sand-dune. She had lost two of them at Luxor airport and the rest had sat in the coach in a state of gathering mutiny. Some of them were given to exclaiming, within her hearing, 'Where's that wretched girl got to?' At Karnak the guide hadn't shown up when he should and she had had to mollify them for half an hour with the shade temperature at 94°. On the boat, a contingent had complained about having cabins on the lower deck and old Mr Appleton, apparently, was on a milk pudding diet, a detail not passed on to the chef by the London office. She knew now that not only did she not like foreign travel or tour leading but she didn't much care for people either. She continued to smile and repeat that they would be able to cash cheques between five and six and that no, she didn't think there was a chiropodist in

Assuan. When several of them succumbed vocifer-
ously to stomach upsets she refrained from saying
that so had she. They sought her out with their
protests and their demands when she was skulking in
a far corner of the sun deck and throughout every
meal. In the privacy of her cabin she drafted her
letter of application to the estate agent in Richmond
where there was a nice secretarial job going.

At Edfu the woman magistrate from Knutsford
was short-changed by a carpet-seller, to the quiet
satisfaction of some of the others. At Esna Miss
Crawley lost her travellers' cheques and Julie had to
go all the way back to the temple and search, amid
the pi-dogs and the vendors of basalt heads and the
American party from Minnesota Institute of Art
(biddable and co-operative, joshing their ebullient
blue-rinsed tour leader). They all called her Julie
now, but on a note of querulous requirement, except
for the retired bank manager, who had tried to grope
her bottom behind a pillar at Kom Ombo, and
followed her around suggesting a drink later on
when his wife was taking a nap.

None of them had read the itinerary properly.
When they discovered that they had an hour and a
half to wait at Assuan for the flight to Abu Simbel

they rounded on her with their objections. They wanted another plane laid on and they wanted to be assured that they wouldn't be with the French and the Japanese tours and Lady Hacking said over and over again that at least one took it, for goodness' sake, that there would be adequate restaurant facilities. She got them, eventually, into the plane and off the plane on to the coach, where the guide, Fuad, promised by the Assuan agency, most conspicuously was not. She went back to the airport building and telephoned; the Assuan office was closed. The man at the EgyptAir desk knew of no Fuad. She returned to the coach and broke the news in her most sprightly manner. The American coach and the French coach and the Japanese coach, smoothly united with their Fuad or their Ashraf, were already descending the long road to the temples in three clouds of dust.

They said their say. The coach driver spat out of the window and closed the door. They bumped across the desert. Lake Nasser lay to their right, bright blue fringed with buff-coloured hills. Those who had sufficiently recovered from their irritation at the non-appearance of Fuad exclaimed. Those who had not continued loudly to reiterate their complaints. The coach driver pulled up at the top of the track down to the temple site. They disembarked. Miss Crawley said she hadn't realised there was going to be even more walking. They straggled off in twos and threes and stood, at last, in front of the blindly gazing immensities of the god-king. Mrs Marriott-Smith said it made you think, despite everything, and Miss Crawley found she had blistered both feet and the chartered surveyor's wife was sorry to tell everyone she couldn't, frankly, see a sign of anywhere to eat. They stood around and took photographs and trailed in the wake of the guided and instructed French and Japanese into the sombre depths of the temple and when they were all out of sight Julie left them.

She walked briskly up the hill to where the American coach, its party already aboard, was revving its engine. She got on and went with them back to the airport, where, with a smile, she deposited an envelope containing twenty-two return halves of Assuan–Abu Simbel–Assuan air tickets with the fellow at the EgyptAir desk. She then boarded the plane, along with the American party. They were shortly joined by the Japanese and the French. The

4 plane left on time; it always did, the stewardess said,

truculently, glancing out of the window at the solitary airport building tipping away beneath.

The Magitours party continued to devote themselves to the site. They gathered in front of the stone plaque unveiled by Gamal Abdul Nasser as a memorial of international collaboration for preserving a human heritage. The other tours were now wending their way up the track to the coaches. 'Peace at last!' said Lady Hacking. 'I don't know which drive me dottier – those American women screaming at each other or the French pushing and shoving.' Mr Campion, the senior police inspector, being in possession of an adequate guide-book, assumed the role of the absent Fuad and briefed them on Rameses the Second and on the engineering feat involved in hoisting the temples to their present position. The party, appropriately humbled by the magnitude of both concepts, moved in awe around the towering pillars of the temple and the equally inhuman twentieth-century shoring-up process within the artificial hillside. They all agreed that it was frightfully impressive and well worth coming for. Those still suffering from internal disorders were becoming a little fidgety, and Mrs Marriott-Smith was longing for her dinner, 5 but on the whole the mood was genial. They emerged from the temple and sat around admiring the lake, tinged now with rose-coloured streaks as the late-afternoon sun sank towards the desert. Some of the women put their woollies on; it was extraordinary how quickly it got chilly in the evenings. Mr Campion read out more from the guide-book. None of them paid any attention to the distant hootings of the coach driver, at the top of the hill. Someone said, 'That damn girl's vanished again.'

The coach driver, hired for so long and no longer, hooted for five minutes. Then, in the absence of any instructions, he threw his cigarette out of the window and drove his empty coach back to the depot.

The sun had almost completely set when the first of them reached the airport building. The stragglers, including the grimly stoical Miss Crawley, now hide-ously blistered, continued to arrive in dribs and drabs for another quarter of an hour. It had been a good two miles. It was Mr Campion who discovered the envelope with the flight tickets, shoved carelessly to one side of the EgyptAir desk. And it was another ten minutes or so, as the party slowly gathered 6 around him, subdued now and in a state of mingled fury and apprehension, before the penny dropped. 'I simply do not believe it,' said the chartered surveyor's wife, over and over again. The EgyptAir official, subjected to a barrage of queries, shrugged, impassive. Those on the edges of the group, who could not quite catch what was going on, pushed closer, and as the enormity of their plight was conveyed from one to another, the murmurs grew louder. Mr Campion, determinedly keeping his cool, concentrated on the EgyptAir fellow. 'When is the next plane, then?' There was not another plane; the last plane left each evening at five-thirty.

'Then,' said Mr Campion with restraint, 'you'll have to call Assuan, won't you, and have them send up another plane.' The EgyptAir official smiled.

'Oh, rubbish,' said Mrs Marriott-Smith. 'Of course they can send another plane. Tell him not to be so silly.' The EgyptAir official shrugged again and made a phone call with the air of a man prepared, up to a point, to placate lunatics. The outcome of the call was clear to all before he put the receiver down.

'All right, then,' said Lady Hacking. 'We shall just have to endure. Ask him where the local hotel is.'

The police inspector, a man accustomed to matters of life and death, did not bother to reply. The 7 woman's manner had been getting on his nerves for days anyway. He simply pointed towards the long windows of the airport building, overlooking a vista of desert enlivened here and there with a scrubby tree or a skulking pi-dog and sliced by the single runway. The sand, now, was lilac, pink and ochre in the sunset. The rest of the group also followed Mr Campion's pointing finger.

'Heavenly colours,' said the Knutsford magistrate. She had tended to display artistic sensibilities since the first morning in Cairo Museum.

The dismay, now, was universal. 'I don't *believe* it,' said the chartered surveyor's wife. 'You'll damn well have to,' snapped her husband. The group, with appalled mutterings, surveyed the uncompromising reality of the airport hall. There were half a dozen rows of solid plastic bucket seats in bright orange, welded to a stone floor with a thick covering of dust, two or three plastic tables, and a soft-drinks counter attended by a young boy who, like the EgyptAir official and the several cleaners or porters, watched them now with mild interest. There was also the EgyptAir desk, on which the official had placed a grubby sign saying CLOSED, some tattered posters on the walls of the Taj Mahal and Sri Lanka, and a great many overflowing rubbish bins. Those who had already sped into the ladies' lavatory had found it awash at one end with urine and attended by a woman who handed each client a dirt-spattered towel and stood expectantly at their sides. Lady Hacking pointed accusingly at the swilling floor; the woman nodded and indicated one of the cubicles from which fumed a trail of sodden toilet paper: 'Is no good.' 'Then *do* something,' said Lady Hacking sternly.

It was now six-thirty. The group, with gathering urgency, had converged on the soft-drinks counter. It was Miss Crawley, a late-comer, who revealed that all that was left were half a dozen cans of 7-Up and four packets of crisps. Those in possession of the only three packets of sandwiches and the single carton of biscuits sat watching, in defiance or guilt according to temperament. 'There are thirteen of us,' announced Miss Crawley loudly, 'without anything at all.' The principle of first come first served was in direct collision now with some reluctant flickerings of community spirit. The two retired librarians offered a sandwich to Mrs Marriott-Smith, who accepted it graciously; they did not offer, it was noted, to anyone else. The temperature had now fallen quite remarkably. The few who had coats put them on; most people shivered in shirt-sleeves and light dresses. The architect who had served in Libya in 1942 reminisced, as he had done before – too often – about the desert campaign. The chartered surveyor's wife told everyone that bloody girl would be bound to get the sack, if that was any comfort. Miss Crawley, with a sigh, took a book from her bag and began ostentatiously to read. A clip-eared white cat lay on one of the plastic tables, luxuriantly squirming. The Knutsford magistrate reached out to stroke it; the cat flexed its claws and opened a red mouth in a soundless mew; Miss Crawley observed without comment.

Outside, it became dark. The EgyptAir official was no longer there. Those sufficiently interested – and resentful – pin-pointed a bungalow at a far corner of the airfield in which lights cosily glimmered. The soft-drinks boy continued to slump at his counter and the ladies' lavatory attendant emerged and squatted on the floor outside. The one remaining porter or watchman came to squat beside her, smoking and exchanging the occasional desultory remark. They ignored the Magitours party, who were now dispersed all over the hall in morose clumps, sitting on the upright bucket seats or leaning against the EgyptAir counter. The architect tried, unsuccessfully, to get together a foursome for whist. Those who were unwell sat near the lavatories, grim-faced. The Knutsford magistrate offered the cat a crumpled ball of newspaper; it lashed out a paw and she withdrew her hand with a squeak.

'I hope it's not rabid,' said Miss Crawley with interest. 'You have to expect that, in places like this.' The magistrate examined her hand, on which beads of blood had appeared. 'Oh *dear* . . .' said Miss Crawley. 'I wonder if it's worth putting on some antiseptic.' The magistrate, glaring, applied Kleenex.

It was at around nine-thirty that the feelings of those without provisions of any kind became insup-portable. The mutiny was provoked by the revelation that the surveyor's wife was in possession of a cache of oranges, Ryvita and Garibaldi biscuits which she now attempted furtively to distribute among those of her choice. The murmurings of those excluded became impossible to ignore; Mr Campion, eventu-ally, rose to his feet, crossed the hall and had a brief and gruff word with the surveyor's wife, who bridled angrily. He then cleared his throat and announced that given the circumstances some kind of a kitty situation as regards food might be a good idea. This produced a small assorted pile which Mrs Campion, with evident embarrassment, divided up and carried round on a tray borrowed from the soft-drinks counter. The several sick said they didn't want anything, prompting further complex and minute division. These comings and goings caused a considerable diversion, so that it was some while before anyone – including his wife – noticed that there was something wrong with old Mr Appleton. He sat slumped down in his seat, intently muttering and emitting, from time to time, a sort of bark that was neither laughter nor a cry of distress. His wife, with as much embarrassment as concern, leaned over him, murmuring exhortations. Presently one of the librarians bustled across with a bottle of mineral water. Aspirins were also produced, and a variety of throat lozenges.

'Poor old chap,' said the Knutsford magistrate. 'Mind, I've been thinking all week he was ever so slightly gaga. What a shame.' Others declared that they weren't surprised – this was enough to unbalance anyone. 'You know what it makes me think of?' said the Knutsford magistrate. 'That place in Orkney – Maeshowe. Anyone been there?' No one had; those for whom she had already over-done the widely

travelled bit returned emphatically to their books or

their magazines. 'Oh, it's quite extraordinary – you really should go. BC three thousand or something but the fascinating thing is these Viking inscriptions by some sailors who spent the night there in a storm and one of them went barmy.' There was a silence. The cat, writhing seductively, wrapped itself round the magistrate's calf; she pushed it away with her bag.

'How does your hand feel?' inquired Miss Crawley.

'Perfectly all right,' said the magistrate with irritation. She watched the cat, which sat lashing its tail. Miss Crawley lowered her book and eyed it. 'Of course all the animals out here look unhealthy. What is that on its mouth?'

At eleven o'clock the only functioning ladies' lavatory packed up, a circumstance causing a frail-looking and hitherto silent woman to burst into ill-concealed sobs. Someone else's husband admitted some amateur plumbing proficiency, rolled up his sleeves and braved the now softly rippling floor. 'Good chap,' said the police inspector loudly.

The attendant at the soft-drinks counter wrapped himself up in a tartan rug, lay down and was seen to fall instantly into deep and tranquil sleep. 'Lucky 13 sod,' said the architect. 'Mind, we used to be able to do that, back on the Halfaya Ridge.'

'Oh, do shut up about the Halfaya Ridge,' said Mrs Marriott-Smith, her voice inadequately lowered. The architect, a more sensitive man than was superficially apparent, and who had shared a genial lunch-table with her and Lady Hacking only yesterday, sat in bristling silence. 'Ssh, dear,' said Lady Hacking. 'Of course, these people aren't made like us physically. It's something to do with their pelvises. Haven't you noticed how they can squat for hours?'

'What absolute nonsense,' muttered the police inspector's wife. Lady Hacking swung round, but was unable to identify the speaker.

The party, by now, had divided into those determinedly enduring in as much isolation as possible and those seeking – tacitly – the faint comfort of collective suffering. One or two had tried to clean up a section of the floor and lie down upon it, inadequately cushioned by newspapers and the contents of handbags, but soon gave up. A few people, drawn to authority, had settled themselves around Mr Campion, as though in wistful belief that he might yet
effect some miracle. Old Mr Appleton continued to

mumble and bark; his wife, now a little wild-eyed, plied him with mineral water.

Mrs Marriott-Smith said, 'Oh my goodness, it *can't* only be half past midnight . . .'

'Tell you what,' said the chartered surveyor's wife. 'We should do community singing. Like people stuck on Scottish mountains.' She giggled self-consciously. 'Don't be so damn silly,' muttered her husband. Miss Crawley, lowering her book, stared with contempt: 'A peculiarly inappropriate analogy, if I may say so.' No one else spoke. The chartered surveyor's wife got out a powder compact and dabbed angrily at her nose.

A detached observer, arriving now at Abu Simbel airport, could not have failed to detect something awry. The complex lines of hostility and aversion linking the members of the Magitours group were like some invisible spider-web, grimly pulsing. Apart from the small group of acolytes around Mr and Mrs Campion, the bucket seats, in their uncompromising welded lines, were occupied in as scattered a manner as possible. Married couples were divided from other married couples by an empty seat or two. Solo travellers like Miss Crawley and the Knutsford magistrate sat in isolation. The two retired librarians had fenced themselves off, pointedly, with a barrier of possessions spread over two unoccupied seats. Old Mr Appleton's barking and muttering had cleared a substantial area around him; he appeared, now, to be asleep, his jaw sagging. From time to time someone would cough, shuffle, murmur to spouse or companion. An uneasy peace reigned, its fragility manifest when someone grated a table against the floor. 'Some of us,' said Lady Hacking loudly, 'are trying to get what rest we can.'

It was at one forty-five that Mr Appleton, apparently, died. He sagged forward and then toppled to the ground with a startling thud, like a mattress dropped from a considerable height. His wife, for a moment or two, did nothing whatsoever; then she began, piercingly, to shriek.

Everyone stood up. Some, like the Campions, the Knutsford magistrate and the librarians, hurried over. Others hovered uncertainly. Miss Crawley, moving to a position where she could see what was going on, said loudly that one must assume a stroke, so there probably wasn't a lot to be done but in any case there was no point in crowding round. Those trying to offer assistance had split into two groups, one devoted to Mr Appleton, the other admonishing his wife, who continued, with quite extraordinary vigour, to scream. 'Hysterics,' said Mrs Marriott-Smith. 'Something I know all about. We had a girl for the children who used to do it, years ago. Someone should slap her face – it's the only thing.'

Mrs Campion, her arm round Mrs Appleton's shoulders, was imploring her to be quiet. 'It's all *right*. Everyone's doing what they can. Do please stop making that noise. *Please*.' Mrs Appleton paused for a moment to draw breath, glanced down at the prone body of her husband, and began again. 'Be quiet!' ordered the inspector. 'Stop that noise!' The librarians and the magistrate were arguing about whether or not to turn Mr Appleton over. 'I tell you, I *know* about this sort of thing – he shouldn't be moved.' 'Excuse me but you're wrong, I know what I'm doing. Is he breathing?' 'I don't think so,' said the magistrate, her words unfortunately falling into a momentary respite in Mrs Appleton's screams, and serving to set her off again nicely.

The soft-drinks attendant had unfurled himself from the tartan rug and, along with the lavatory attendant and the porter, stood watching with interest. 'Tell them to get a doctor,' said Lady Hacking. 'I should think that's the best thing to do.'   17

'Shut up, for Christ's sake, you stupid woman,' said the police inspector. There was a startled silence; even Mrs Appleton, briefly, was distracted. Lady Hacking went brick red and turned her back. The chartered surveyor's wife burst into frenzied laughter. The Knutsford magistrate, kneeling over Mr Appleton, looked up and snapped that she didn't frankly see what there was to laugh about just at the moment. Mrs Appleton had been led to a seat somewhat apart and was being damped down, with some success, by Mrs Campion. Mr Campion, having picked up the receiver of the phone on the EgyptAir desk and listened for a moment, was trying to convey to the porter that the EgyptAir official must be summoned. 'Is sleeping,' said the porter. 'Office closed.' 'Give him some baksheesh,' advised the architect. The police inspector, a big man, ignored this; he leaned forward, seized the porter's jacket in either hand, and violently shook him. The lavatory attendant uttered a shrill cry of outrage.

'Frightfully unwise,' said Mrs Marriott-Smith loudly. 'That simply isn't how to deal with these people.' Interest, now, was diverted from the Appletons to the EgyptAir counter.

The porter, muttering angrily, picked up the phone, and, presently, was heard to speak into it. 'Tell him to bloody well get over here at once,' said Mr Campion, 'and bloody well get on to Assuan for us.'

'The man doesn't understand English,' said Miss Crawley.

'At least some of us are trying to *do* something,' hissed the magistrate. 'Which is more than can be said for others.'

Miss Crawley stared, icily: 'There's no need to be offensive.'

Lady Hacking, tight-lipped, was sitting stiffly while Mrs Marriott-Smith spoke in a mollifying undertone. 'I have no intention,' said Lady Hacking loudly, 'of getting involved. One simply ignores such behaviour, is what one does.' The chartered surveyor's wife gazed at her, beady-eyed.

The porter had put down the phone and was loudly reiterating his grievances. 'All right, all right, old chap,' said the engineer. 'We've got the message. Calm down.' Mrs Appleton continued keening; Mrs Campion, still in attendance, was becoming visibly impatient. The woman who had been reduced to tears by the collapse of the surviving ladies' lavatory was again quietly weeping. 'I just want to be at home,' she kept saying. 'That's all. I want to go home.'

At this point Mr Appleton twitched convulsively and made an attempt to roll on to his back. 'He's coming round,' announced the magistrate. 'Good grief! I thought he'd croaked, between you and me.' The librarians, with cries of encouragement, heaved him into a sitting position.

The porter, shrugging, looked meaningfully at Mr Campion: 'Is OK now.' 'Go to hell,' said the police inspector, advancing towards Mr Appleton, who was heard to ask where he was. 'Don't tell him,' advised the engineer. 'It'll be enough to knock the poor fellow out again.'

Mrs Appleton, supported by Mrs Campion, was led across to her husband and began attempting to brush the dust off his trousers and jacket while reproaching him for giving everyone such a nasty shock. The old man, ignoring her, allowed himself to be helped up into a seat; he stared round, wheezing. 'That's the ticket,' said the police inspector, patting him on the shoulder.

The EgyptAir official arrived, tie-less and with one shirt-tail untucked. The porter fell on him in noisy complaint. The police inspector, cutting in, took him aside. 'Spot of baksheesh might save the situation,' said the architect. Mr Campion continued, in quiet but authoritative tones, to explain that a member of the party had been taken ill, and was undoubtedly in need of medical attention, but that fortunately the immediate crisis seemed to have passed. 'Man not dead,' stated the EgyptAir official, aggrievedly. 'No, I'm happy to say,' said Mr Campion.

And when, presently, dawn broke over the desert and a grey light crept into the airport building the scene there was one of, if not peace, at least an exhausted truce. A few of the Magitours party, done for, were in restless sleep; the others, raw-eyed, sat staring out of the windows at the reddening desert or braved the lavatories to attempt whatever might be done by way of physical repairs. The librarians graciously offered cologne-soaked tissues. A few people ventured outside for a breath of air and even wandered a little way along the road to the temples, at the far end of which those stone immensities, in their solitude, were contemplating yet another sunrise.

And when, three hours later, the first flight from

Assuan decanted its passengers the arrivals found the place occupied by a party of people grim-faced but composed. Members of a Cook's tour bore down on them: 'I say, is it true you've been here all night? It must have been ghastly!' Those who saw fit to respond were deprecating. 'The odd little contretemps,' said Lady Hacking graciously. 'But on the whole we muddled through quite nicely.' Miss Crawley, in sepulchral tones, warned of the condition of the lavatories. The librarians, gaily, said it had been a bit like an air-raid in the war, if you were old enough to remember. Mrs Appleton, supporting her husband, who was demanding a morning paper, valiantly smiled. The wan appearance of the party was defied by an air of determined solidarity, even perhaps of reticence. 'The thing was,' said the Knutsford magistrate, 'we were all in the same boat, so there was nothing for it but grin and bear it.' The exclamations and queries of the Cook's tour members were parried with understated evasions. Mrs Marriott-Smith assured the new arrivals that the temples were absolutely amazing, unforgettable, no question about that. 'Absolutely,' said the police inspector heartily. 'Extraordinary place.' There was a murmur of agreement and, as the Cook's tour filed towards their coach, the Magitours party, rather closely clumped together, made their way across the sand-strewn tarmac to the waiting plane.

The Emasculation of Ted Roper

Jeanie Banks, rigid with emotion, her cardigan on inside out, muttering rehearsed words, deaf and blind to the bright morning, made her way down the village street. Past the post office, the one, two, three, four cottages, past the pub, Mrs Halliday's, the garage, the one, two, three new bungalows, the Lathams', Cardwell's yard. She stopped outside Roper's, simmering, reached out to open the gate, lost her nerve, plunged on down to the lamp-post where the village ended, yanked up her resolution again, turned, aimed back, fumbled furious with the latch on Roper's gate.

The front garden a disgrace, as always, strewn with empty oil cans, plastic sacks, rusting iron objects, the excretions of Roper's hand-to-mouth odd-jobbing dealing-in-this-and-that existence. Furtive, unreliable, transacting in dirty pound notes, dodging his taxes without a doubt, down the pub every evening. Dirty beggar, cocky as a robin, sixty if he was a day.

Feeling swelled to a crescendo, and courage with it; she hammered on the door. Then again. And again. No answer. He'd be there all right, he'd be there, nine-thirty in the morning, since when did Roper go out and do a decent day's work? She shoved at the side gate.

He was round the back, fiddling about with a great pile of timber, good timber at that, planks all sizes and shapes and how did he come by it one would like to know? A whole lot of tyres stacked up in one corner, stuff spilling out of the shed, filth everywhere.

'Hello, Jeanie.'

She halted, breathless now. Words fail you, they do really. They leave you huffing and puffing, at a disadvantage, seeing suddenly the run in your tights, seeing yourself reflected in the eyes of others – angry, dumpy, middle-aged widow, just Jeanie Banks. In the beady spicy nasty eyes of Ted Roper, stood there in the middle of his junk like a little farmyard cock. A randy strutting bantam cock.

'What can I do for you, Jeanie?'

She said, 'It's not what you can do it's what's been done, that's what's the trouble.'

'Trouble?' He took out tobacco, a grubby roll of cigarette papers. 'Trouble?' His dirty fingers, rolling, tapping, his tongue flickering over the paper.

'My Elsa's expecting.'

'Expecting?' he said. 'Oh – expecting.' A thin smile now, a thin complacent smile. Grinning away at it, the old bastard, pleased as punch. As if it were something to be proud of, as if it did him credit even, stood there with his thumbs stuck in his trouser pockets like those boys in western films. Some boy – Ted Roper. Boy my foot, sixty if he's anything.

'That's what I said. Expecting.'

He put the cigarette in his mouth; thin smoke fumed into the village sunshine. Not trousers, she saw now. Jeans – jeans just like young men wear, slumped down on his thin hips, the zip sliding a bit, a fullness you couldn't miss below, stuck out too the way he stood, legs apart, thumbs in pockets.

'Well,' he said, 'I s'pose that'd be in the nature of things. She's getting a big girl now.'

Grinning away there, wiry and perky and as blatant as you like. She felt her outrage surge.

26   'It's rape,' she said. 'That's what it damn well is.

A little creature like that, a little young thing. Bloody rape!' The colour rushed to her cheeks; she didn't use language like that, not she, never.

'Now, now, Jeanie. Who's to know who gave who the come on.'

She exploded. She shouted, 'You take that blasted cat to the vet, Ted Roper, and get it seen to, the rest of us have just about had enough, there's kittens from one end of the village to the other and my Elsa was nothing but a kitten herself.' She swung round and stormed to the gate. When she looked back he was still standing there, the cigarette laid on his lower lip, his jeans fraying at the crotch, the grin still on his face. 'Or you'll find it done for you one of these days!'

All the way back to the cottage her heart thumped. It didn't do you any good, getting yourself into a state like that, it took it out of you, she'd be jumpy all day now. Back home in the kitchen, she made herself a cup of tea. The old cat, the mother, was sprawled in the patch of sun on the mat and Elsa was in the armchair. When Jeanie came in she jumped down and shimmied across the floor: pretty, graceful, kittenish and distinctly lumpy, no doubt about it, that unmistakable pear-shape forming at the end of

her. And Jeanie, subsiding into the chair, drinking
her tea, eyed her and eyed the old cat, not so old
come to that, five or was it six, and as she did so a
whole further implication leaped into the mind –
why hadn't she thought of it before, how disgusting,
if it were people you could have them slapped in
prison for that.

'Fact is,' said her sister Pauline, that afternoon,
'there's probably hardly a one in the village isn't his.
Being the only tom round about, bar him on Lay's
farm and he's beyond it if you ask me. So you let
Ted Roper have it? Good on you, Jeanie.'

Jeanie, cooler now, calmer, righteous and ever so
slightly heroic, went over it all again, word for word:
I said, he said, so I said, and him as cocky as you
like.

'He's a cocky little so-and-so,' said Pauline.
'Always was. I bet he got the wind up a bit though,
Jeanie, with you bawling him out, you're bigger than
he is.' She chuckled. 'Hey – d'you remember the
time they got him in the girls' playground and
Marge ripped the belt off his trousers so he had to
hold 'em up all afternoon? God – laugh . . .! Donkey's
years ago . . .'

'Funny, isn't it,' Pauline went on, 'there's four of

us in the village still as were at school with Ted. You, me, Nellie Baker, Marge. Randy he was, too. Remember?'

'Funny he's never married,' said Jeanie.

Pauline snorted. 'Out for what he can get, that one. Not that he'd get it that often, is my guess.'

'Can't stand the man. Never could. 'Nother cup? Anyway, what I say is, he ought to be made to have something done about that cat. It's shocking. Shocking.'

In the basket chair the old cat raucously purred; Elsa, in a patch of sunlight, lay flirting with a length of string.

'Sick of drowning kittens, I am,' said Jeanie. 'I'll have to get her seen to after, like I did the old cat. Shame.'

'Shame.'

The two women contemplated the cats.

'I mean, we wouldn't care for it, if it were you or me.'

'Too right.'

'Not,' said Pauline, 'at that time of life. That's a young creature, that is, she's got a right to, well, a right to things.'

'Hysterectomy's the nearest, if it were a person.' 29

'That's it, Jeanie. And you'd not hear of that if it were a girl. Another matter if it's in middle life.'

'That cat of Roper's,' said Jeanie, 'must be going on twelve or thirteen.'

Later, as she walked to the shop, Roper's pick-up passed her, loaded with slabs of timber, belting too fast down the village street, Roper at the wheel, one arm on the sill, a young lad beside him, one of the several who hung around him. She saw Roper see her, turn to the boy, say something, the two of them roar grinning across the cross-roads. She stood still, seething.

'Cardwell's boy, weren't that?' said Marge Tranter, stopping also. 'With Roper.'

'I daresay. What they see in that old devil . . .'

'Men's talk. Dirty stories, that stuff. Norman says he doesn't half go on in the pub, Roper. He's not a one for that kind of thing, Norman isn't. He says Roper holds out hours on end sometimes, sat there in the corner with his mates. Showing off, you know.'

'Fat lot he's got to show off about,' said Jeanie. 'A little runt, he is. Always was. I was saying to Pauline, remember the time you . . .'

'Pulled his trousers down, wasn't it? Don't remind me of that, Jeanie, I'll die . . .'

'Not pulled them down, it wasn't. Took his belt. Anyway, Marge, I gave him an earful this morning, I'll tell you that. That cat of his has been at my Elsa. I went straight down there and I said look here, Ted Roper . . .'

A quarter of a mile away Ted Roper's pick-up, timber dancing in the back, dodged in and out of the traffic on the A34, overtaking at sixty, cutting in, proving itself. Cardwell's boy and Roper, blank-faced, be-jeaned, the cowboys of the shires, rode the Oxfordshire landscape.

In the village and beyond, Roper's cat – thin, rangy, one-eyed and fray-eared – went about his business.

And, according to the scheme of things, the ripe apples dropped from the trees, the *jeunesse dorée* of the area switched their allegiance from the Unicorn to the Hand and Shears taking with them the chattering din of un-muffled exhausts and the reek of high-octane fuel, the road flooded at the railway bridge and Jeanie's Elsa swelled soft and sagging like the bag of a vacuum cleaner.

'Several at least,' said Jeanie. 'Half a dozen, if you ask me. Poor little thing, it's diabolical.'

'There's a side to men,' said Pauline, 'that's to my 31

mind just not like us and that's the only way you can put it. And I don't mean sex, nothing wrong with that when the time and the place are right. I mean . . .'

'It's a kind of men rather, I'd say. Harry's not that way, nor was my Jim. I mean, there's men that are normal men in the proper way but don't go on about it.'

'In Italy,' said Pauline, 'all the men are the other kind. All of them. From the word go. Young boys and all. They wear bathing costumes cut deliberately so you can see everything they've got.'

'Which is something you can take as read, in a normal man. It doesn't need shouting about.'

'Exactly. If I were you, Jeanie, I'd give that cat a drop of cod liver oil in her milk. She's going to need all her strength.'

Perhaps also according to the scheme of things, Ted Roper's pick-up, a while later, was involved in circumstances never clarified in a crash with Nellie Baker's Escort at the village cross-roads. No blood was shed and the pick-up, already so battle-scarred as to be impervious, lived to fight again, but the Escort was crippled and Nellie Baker too shaken and confused to be able to sort out exactly what had happened except for a strong conviction that aggression had been involved. At the Women's Institute committee meeting she held forth.

'He came out of nowhere and was into me before I knew what was happening. I was either stopped or the next best thing, that I'll swear.'

'What does he say?'

'Whatever he's saying's being said to the police. He took off, without a word hardly. It was Mr Latham ran me home and got the garage for me. I've told them my side of it, at the police station. It's up to them now.'

'The police,' said Jeanie Banks, 'have been down at Ted Roper's more than once. Asking about this and that. They could do some asking just now, the stuff he's got there and one wonders where it all comes from.'

'The police,' said Pauline, 'are men. Remember Ted Roper at school, Nellie? Jeanie and I were talking about that only the other day – how we used to take him down a peg or two.'

And, according to a scheme of things or not, no case was brought against Ted Roper for careless driving or dangerous driving or aggression or anything at all. Those who failed to see how that pick-up 33 could have passed its MOT continued to speculate; Ted Roper's insurance company ignored letters from Nellie Baker's insurance company.

Jeanie's Elsa had five kittens, two of them stillborn.

Ted Roper, wiry and self-assured as his cat, continued to cruise the local roads, to make his corner of the pub an area of masculine assertion as impenetrable and complacent as the Athenaeum. From it came gusts of hoarse laughter and anecdotes which were not quite audible, bar certain key words.

It may have been the stillborn kittens that did it, as much as anything, those damp limp little rags of flesh. Or the sight of the emptied Elsa, restored to a former litheness but subtly altered, wise beyond her years. Or months.

Jeanie, tight-lipped, visited Marge to borrow her cat basket.

'You'll take her to be done, then?'

'Have to, won't I? Or it'll be the same thing over again.'

'Shame.'

'Just what Pauline said.'

Marge, lining the cat basket with a piece of old blanket, paused. 'It's like with people. Always taken for granted it must be the woman. Pills, messing about with your insides . . .' She swung the door of the basket shut and tested the catch. 'There's an alternative, Jeanie. Thought of that?'

'What do you think I was down Ted Roper's for, that time?'

'And much joy you got out of it. No, what I'm thinking of is we see to it ourselves.'

The two women stared at each other over the cat basket. Marge, slowly, even rather terribly, smiled. 'I wouldn't mind, I wouldn't half mind, giving Ted Roper his come uppance.'

In a village, people come and go all day. Women, in particular – to and from the school, the shop, the bus stop, each other's houses. The little group of Jeanie, Pauline, Marge and Nellie Baker, moving in a leisurely but somehow intent way around the place that afternoon, glancing over garden walls and up the sides of cottages, was in no way exceptional. Nor, unless the observer were of a peculiarly inquiring turn of mind, was the fact that they carried, between them, a cat basket, a pair of thick leather gardening gloves, and a half a pound of cod wrapped in newspaper.

Presently, the cat basket now evidently heavy and

bouncing a little from side to side, they emerged somewhat breathless from the field behind the pub and made their way rather hurriedly to the garage of Nellie Baker's house, where an old Morris replaced the deceased Escort. The Morris drove away in the direction of Chipping Norton passing, incidentally, the very school playground where once, donkey's years ago, four outraged and contemptuous school-girls had a go at the arrogance of masculine elitism.

In a village, also, change is more quickly observed than you might think. Even change so apparently insignificant as the girth of a cat. In this case, it was habits as much as girth. A cat that has previously roamed and made the night hideous, and which takes instead to roosting, eyes closed and paws folded, in the sun on the tops of walls, idling away the time, will be noticed.

And the more so when the change eerily extends to the cat's owner.

At first it was just the paunch jutting below the sagging belt of Ted Roper's jeans. Then, balancing the paunch, came a fullness to the face, a thickening of the stubbly cheeks, a definite double chin. 'Put on a bit, haven't you, Ted?' people said. 'Have to cut down on the beer, eh?' And Ted would wryly grin, without the perky come-back that might have been expected. With physical expansion went a curious decline of those charismatic qualities: the entourage of youths dropped off. Some nights, Ted sat alone in the pub, staring into his glass with the ruminative and comfortably washed-up look of his seniors. A series of mishaps befell the pick-up: punctures stranding Ted on remote roads, a catastrophic fuel leak, a shattered windscreen. It was driven, presently, in a more sedate way; it no longer rode or cruised but rattled and pottered.

It was as though the old assertive stringy cocky Ted were devoured and enveloped, week after week, by this flabby amiable lethargic newcomer. The jeans gave way to a pair of baggy brown cords. He began to leave his corner of the public bar and join the central group around the fireplace; there, the talk was of onions, the ills of the nation, weather and fuel prices.

And, in the village or outside his own gate, meeting Nellie Baker, say, or Marge or Pauline or Jeanie Banks, he would pass the time of day, initiate a bit of chat, offer small gifts by way of surplus timber, useful lino offcuts, the odd serviceable tyre.

'Poor old so-and-so,' said Pauline. 'They're easily 37

taken down, aren't they? That's what comes of depending on the one thing. You can almost feel sorry for them.'

Pack of Cards

She caused him sleepless nights. He lay awake lusting after her, aflame for her, the darkened room full of her voice and her face and her round full limbs. He would get up and open the window in the hope that cooling night air might do something for him; he would put on the light and reach for a book. Books were definitely therapeutic, certain books; it was a new insight into the function of literature. You needed something familiar, but with abiding power. The Russians were best. Turgenev. Chekhov. He stilled the flesh with *Home of the Gentry* and *Spring Torrents.* Which she of course would not have read; most certainly would not have read.

She worked as receptionist at a firm of management consultants. She sat amid rubber plants and deep leather chairs answering the phone in her clear confident tone; she processed visitors from the leather chairs to the offices of the consultants, varnished young men with the same sort of voice. He knew those voices; he had heard them in his childhood, in the shops of Suffolk market towns, at point-to-points and later, of course, at Oxford. Five-pound note voices, his mother used to call them. Voices that survived wars and revolutions, ringing down the years; you could not but feel a certain admiration.

How he came to be in thrall to such a voice he could not think; considered dispassionately, it set his teeth on edge. If he closed his eyes sanity returned – almost. But then, opening them, he saw her round flawless face, her ashy silken hair, her flesh . . . ah, her flesh, into which he longed to sink his teeth as though into a peach – no, a nectarine, a golden pink-stained juice-rich nectarine . . . And to hell with the voice. And with what it said.

'Honestly, I don't know *what* I see in you . . .' Accompanied by a peck on the cheek, a pat, some propitiatory gesture. In bed, it told him he was dreadful, awful, really she must be mad, she couldn't think what she was doing. And when he informed her (she was twenty-five, after all, it was time she put a name to these things, called a spade a spade) she would put her hand over his mouth and bury her face in his neck, giggling. 'Stop it!' she would say. 'Nick, I absolutely forbid . . . I'm not listening, right?'

She was always busy, about to dash off somewhere – for the weekend, or to meet this old old friend, or to get her hair seen to. And when she wasn't she was far too expensive for him: Ronnie Scott's, cocktail bars, theatres. She told him he absolutely must get a car, just something second-hand, a silly little Renault or something, and when he said he couldn't afford one she stared at him and laughed uncertainly. When, occasionally, she introduced him to her friends, she stressed his eccentricity. 'Nick's so *clever*,' she said. 'He's got this extraordinary job on some magazine that sells about ten copies because it's too brilliant for anyone to understand.' And the friends rolled their eyes and murmured. 'He's your original intellectual, he simply does not care about *things*. He can live absolutely anyhow, isn't he marvellous!'; and the friends smiled indulgently, or not. He was a pet, he saw – an intriguing, amusing, faintly disturbing *divertissement*. Sometimes she hinted at inadequacies of dress or behaviour. She gave him an expensive sweater, which he lost. She wished he'd get out of that grotty bed-sitter and find a proper flat – it would be easy to fix up a mortgage, her godfather was head of a building society. When she met his friends she was bright and gracious and said 41 afterwards that she couldn't think *quite* why he hung around with people like that, of course they were interesting in a way but.

He assumed, in calmer moments, that it would pass. In the meantime there was nothing for it but to burn.

She said, 'You've got to meet Granny. You'll adore her. Now she really is absolutely your cup of tea. She's a real book lady. She's the literary person in our family. *Her* mother, you see, Great-Granny – not that I ever knew her she died before I was born – anyway she was part of a sort of set, famous writers and people, she knew absolutely everyone. She's got letters from Galsworthy and Tennyson and people. Granny has, I mean.'

'Tennyson?' he said.

'I think so. Anyway, that sort of person. Granny's got an amazing library. You'll be frightfully impressed. She's a terrific character. Anyway, we're all going down there for lunch on Sunday – we go once a month, everyone – and it's O.K. for you to come.'

'Where?' he said.

'Henley, of course. Daddy'll drive us.'

Her father was a director of one of those companies whose function is so abstruse that they appear to exist only in order to manage money, unassociated with anything so mundane as a specific product – oil or bricks or shoes or soapflakes. There would also be, she explained, her uncle Dickie who was in banking, and his wife, and Mummy of course, and another uncle who was with Cluttons, and *his* wife. And some cousins.

'Cluttons? The estate agents?'

'Well – property people, really. Anyway, you'll come with us and they'll all be going separately. Oh, and it's usually tidyish sort of clothes, for Granny. I don't mean a suit. Just sort of casual tidy, see?'

He saw, arriving at her house: her father in well-creased trousers and crisp open-neck shirt straight from the window of Simpsons. Mummy in something trim and silky. He had met them once before; they greeted him this time with just a shade too much fervour. Her father had the bonnet of the car open; 'Sorry, Nick – can't shake you by the hand, oil everywhere. Good to see you. Excellent. Couple of minutes and we'll be off. Why don't you and Charlotte go in the back together?' The car bonnet dropped with the clunk of expensive engineering. 'Ever been in one of these?'

Nick said he hadn't.

'Ah. Well, I think you'll find it rather fun. This is the new model, of course. Fuel injection, power-assisted steering, hydraulic engine mounting – the works. Great fun to drive. You keen on driving?'

Nick said he wasn't.

'Ah. Well. When I was your age I had an old Lancia. Did about ten to the gallon – absurd motor-car for a penniless young man. Great fun, though. Right – all here, are we? Let's go, then – there'll be hell to pay if we keep mother waiting.'

In the car Charlotte patted the knee of his trousers with what he recognised as an admonitory gesture. The trousers were not clean. He had intended to wash them but had left it too late. His shirt was clean but unironed. He shifted his knee slightly and gazed at the back of Charlotte's mother's head, of which each hair appeared to have been separately arranged. Charlotte removed her hand from his knee, slid it into his and tickled his palm. London slid soundlessly past; white stucco, black railings and polished doorknockers gave way to hoardings advertising whisky and airlines. From time to time Charlotte's father pressed switches; windows moved up or down, water sprayed on to the windscreen, air discreetly blew.

'Let's see now, Nick – what's your line? Can't quite remember. Journalism – that right?'

Nick explained.

'Interesting, I should imagine,' said Charlotte's father after a moment. 'And where d'you go from there, then?'

Nick said he hadn't thought much about that.

They reached the motorway. Charlotte leaned forward. 'Do a hundred, Daddy, go on!'

'Don't be silly, darling,' said her mother.

'Not with the sort of idiots there are around. Besides, too early won't do either. You know your grandmother.' The father raised his voice slightly, for Nick's benefit, as though he might be slightly deaf. 'My mother's something of a grand old lady – I daresay Charlotte's told you. Remarkable woman. Keeps up her own mother's tradition. The literary connection.'

'She knew all sorts of famous writers,' said Charlotte's mother, 'Galsworthy and um . . . Kipling, was it? And . . .'

'Tennyson?' said Nick.

'Oh, I'm sure,' said the mother.

'Amazing library,' said Charlotte's father. 'I daresay you'll get a look round.'

'Ah . . .'

'You'll be interested. More up your street than some of Charlotte's friends.'

'Oh, shut up, Daddy,' said Charlotte.

'Keep your hair on, sweetie. No one's criticising. Tell the truth, Nick, I'm not a great reader myself. The odd Len Deighton, that sort of thing. Mother's in a different league. Wonderful collection of books. Extremely valuable, of course.'

'That house is just stuffed,' said the mother. 'What's to be done eventually one hates to think.'

'I'm *starving*,' cried Charlotte. 'I hope it's not going to be sherry for hours before we eat.' She rubbed the back of her hand against Nick's thigh. He wondered why he was not getting an erection; perhaps speed inhibited the libido in some curious way.

They arrived, turning sharply off the road into a concealed entrance, down a driveway and out on to a precise circle of creamy gravel bordered by a ring of mown grass and high, scrupulously clipped hedges. Tubs of geraniums stood around. A flight of steps led up to the front door. The house was large, architecturally undistinguished and of the inter-war years. Very clean cars in unusual colours were parked on the gravel, as though displayed for advertising purposes. Charlotte's mother, getting out, said, 'Oh lor – we're the last.'

They went through to a large drawing-room overlooking the garden, in which a dozen or so people stood holding glasses. There were cries and embraces. Charlotte led him round: 'This is Nick ... Hello, Aunt Frances – oh, fantastic – Jamie's here!' They were all sleek and glowing, like animals fed and groomed to show condition; the older men shook him by the hand, the women smiled, the young said, 'Oh, hello . . .'

On a sofa sat the old woman – small, with a dowager's hump. Charlotte said, 'Granny, here's Nick who we told you about.' He held out his hand and she took it and then dropped it at once. She stared at him for a moment and turned to Charlotte's father: 'You're late, Rupert.'

'Ten minutes, mother. Traffic the London end. Sorry.'

'Well, we'll go in and eat. Tell them in the kitchen.' She began to heave herself up; sons sprang forward. 'No, leave me alone, I can manage. Get the rest of them through to the dining-room. I want Dickie next to me, and Clarissa. Put Charlotte's young man somewhere near – I'll talk to him. Is he the one who's something to do with some magazine?'

A huge oblong mahogany table, glinting with silver and cut glass; dark oil paintings on the walls (dead pheasants, bowls of sheeny fruit, Stubbs-looking animals); thick carpets and a smell of roast meat. They were disposed around the table by one of the women – 'You there, Charlotte, and um, Nick beside you, and I'll go here and what about Jamie and Sue over the other side ...' Girls in aprons whisked in and out carrying dishes; Charlotte's father stood at a sideboard sharpening a carving-knife.

The old woman sat hunched at the head of the table, unfurling a white napkin, talking loudly to a daughter-in-law half-way down. Charlotte shouted to a cousin at the far end about a party she'd been to. An uncle – the estate agent or the banker? – was talking about something he'd bought (house? factory? set of golf clubs?). Caught in the crossfire of several conversations, Nick pondered the warring snatches; everything was referential, named names, specified: 'Those last catering people were no good so I've sacked them. These girls are from Binneys in Maidenhead. What's that meat like, Rupert?' ... 'Lucy and Camilla were there, and both the Warrington boys, and the band was fantastic' ... 'So I got them down from frankly a silly price to something worth talking about and if Handley okays it I think we may well be in business.' One of the aunts, a clone it seemed to him of Charlotte's mother, leaned across the table and said, 'Do you know this part of the world at all, Nick?' Did she take him for a foreigner? But no, the reference was purely local, it seemed – she was talking about Henley; 'Mother thinks it's quite ruined, of course, since her day, but actually it's really very civilised still.'

Each time the old woman made some remark at large they all quietened in deference, smiled indulgently at her pronouncements.

'What's that peculiar outfit Charlotte's wearing? The colours swear appallingly.'

'Granny! It cost the earth!'

'I daresay. The latest thing, I suppose. I never went chasing after fashion when I was your age. I had good clothes and they lasted me for years. Of course mother had such marvellous taste.'

'There's a portrait of Great-Granny in the library,' murmured Charlotte. 'I'll show you later. She was gorgeous when she was young.'

'What are you talking about, Charlotte?'

'I was telling Nick I'll show him Great-Granny's portrait after lunch.'

Mrs Lavington fixed him with her small, black, glittery eyes. 'What is it you do?'

'I work as editorial assistant on a journal.'

'What sort of journal?'

'An academic journal. It's called the *English Language Critical Quarterly*. The editor was my tutor at Oxford.'

The table had fallen silent.

'What college?' demanded Mrs Lavington.

'St Edmund Hall.'

'My husband was at Magdalen. Apparently Oxford isn't up to much nowadays.'

'Really?' said Nick.

'No. It's gone to pot completely. My sons didn't go there.'

'Not intellectual types like you and father,' said Rupert Lavington. 'Anyone want another slice off the joint? Second helps?'

Mrs Lavington was still fixed on Nick. 'What do they pay you?'

'Sorry?'

'At this magazine. What do they pay you?'

'Granny!' said Charlotte.

'Six thousand a year.'

A ripple of embarrassment ran round the table. 'I think I *will* have some more,' said Charlotte's mother. 'Come on, Clarissa, keep me company.'

'God!' said the youngest male cousin. 'I don't know how you manage. I'm on eight and a half and I'm always skint.'

Nick considered Mrs Lavington. She made him think of the tortoise he had had when he was ten: the wrinkled neck, the small head on the end of it turning slowly this way and that. He watched her eat and remembered the tortoise (whose name was Fred) – lettuce leaves withdrawn half inch by half inch with each deliberate crunch of horny jaws, occasional glimpses of a grey tongue. He had liked Fred; he did not care for Mrs Lavington at all.

'Nick's like you, Granny,' said Charlotte. 'He's a terrific reader. He's got hundreds of books. All over the floor mostly in his crazy room. Paperbacks, of course.'

The old woman stared down the table at him. 'I can't stand a paperback. I've got to have a properly bound book. I can't bear to go into a bookshop nowadays, all those garish covers screaming at you. I always ordered everything from Bumpus. I don't expect you've ever heard of Bumpus?'

'No.'

'It's gone now. When my mother went there they used to put out the red carpet. Old Mr Bumpus always served her himself.'

'Aren't books a price nowadays!' said one of the daughters-in-law. 'Proper books. I got that David Attenborough wild life thing the other day for Timmie. Fifteen pounds!'

Mrs Lavington's reptilean head swung round. 'I was talking about my mother, Clarissa.'

The daughter-in-law, rebuked, patted her mouth with her napkin.

'Galsworthy once told my mother that her collection was one of the finest he'd seen. There is a Nonsuch Shakespeare. I don't imagine you've ever seen a Nonsuch Shakespeare?'

'No,' said Nick. 'I haven't.'

'And of course a large number of first editions. My mother was interested in modern writing also. Arnold Bennett always asked her to read his work before publication.'

'And Tennyson?' inquired Nick.

Mrs Lavington, who had just put a forkful of food

into her mouth, chewed, eyeing him. Around the table, there were rustlings; people cleared their throats, applied themselves to food, embarked on new conversations. Mrs Lavington, her mouth finally empty, said, 'Growing up in a house with an outstanding collection makes all the difference. Books are one's world.'

'Are your people frightfully bookish, Nick?' asked Charlotte's mother. He reflected. Mrs Lavington's cold eye was still on him. He said, 'They don't have all that many books. We always used the public library a lot.'

Mrs Lavington glittered; she almost smiled. 'I have never been into a public library.'

Plates were cleared. An apple tart with cream was served. The conversation turned to choice of holiday destinations, the wedding of a relative, the price of stereo equipment. The format appeared to be not so much an exchange of views and information, or a process whereby someone said something which prompted an addition or comment from someone else, but everyone saying whatever came into their head. The dog-leg effect was peculiarly disorienting. From time to time Mrs Lavington would slice into the middle of someone's statement 53 with a pronouncement, not relevant. Nick sat silent; he could see no point in adding to all this. When, at last, everyone had finished eating, Mrs Lavington said, 'Tell those girls to serve coffee in the library,' and began to grind her chair backwards; sons, again, leapt to her aid and were waved away.

Out in the hall, the women trooped upstairs, chatting. The men stood about, lighting cigars. They were all large and extremely clean; Nick had been noticing, during the meal, the manicured hands around him, nails cut level and scrubbed. Charlotte often picked his hands up and made a little face.

She was waiting now at the foot of the stairs. 'Just going up to powder our noses. The men's loo is that door there. What do you think of Granny – isn't she a character!' The others had gone through the open double doors at the end of the hall. Charlotte leaned up against him and nuzzled his neck. 'Mmn . . . Enjoying yourself?'

'Yes,' he said, 'I rather think I might be.' She was still nuzzling; interestingly, he found himself once more inert.

She peered at him. 'Well, that's a funny way of putting it.'

He moved away. 'I think I'll have a pee.'

He came out of the lavatory and washed his hands in a washroom liberally equipped with fluffy towels and new pieces of soap. Charlotte's father came in. 'Ah, Nick ... Excellent. Coffee on offer in the library when you're ready. Chance for you to take a look at the famous collection.'

The library was as large as the drawing-room; the walls were panelled, and lined with glass-fronted bookcases. They were all there, sitting about on leather sofas or perched on the arms of the chairs. As he came in Charlotte's mother was saying to one of the other women, 'Oh no, not serious we hope. You know Charlotte – always prone to passing fancies . . .' She looked up, broke off and flashed a smile: 'Coffee on the side, Nick, we just help ourselves.'

He poured a cup of coffee and began to move along in front of the bookcases. Everything in sets – leather-bound, gold-tooled. Complete works of everyone. The Nonsuch Shakespeare. Nothing antiquarian. Everything circa 1910, by the look of it. He tried to open a glass door; it was locked. One of the uncles came forward; 'Having a look at the books? Quite an impressive sight.'

'I was trying to open the case,' said Nick. 'It seems to be locked.'

'Oh, I imagine it would be, yes. Mother'll know where the keys are. Mother! Nick here wanted to have a squint at some of the books.'

Mrs Lavington, sunk into the depths of an armchair, glared across the room. 'Why?'

'I wondered if the Dickens was Phiz or Cruikshank.'

'I can't look out the keys just at this moment. Those cases over there are open.'

He crossed the room. Here, the glass was of the lift-up kind – raise the panel and slide it back into the groove above the shelf; a cumbersome process not conducive to easy browsing. He put his coffee down and began to investigate. Kipling, red morocco edition, 1920. He took out *Plain Tales from the Hills*; the spine had the stiffness of a new book, the flimsy India paper pages clung together. He put it back and tried *Kim*; again, the creaking spine and tacky edges of an unopened book. He moved from shelf to shelf, sampled Trollope, Hardy, Meredith, Tennyson (aha! Tennyson ... stout brown calf gilt Gothic-lettered definitely virgin Tennyson); an invoice for ten shillings and sixpence (Bumpus, Booksellers, Oxford Street) fell out of *A Passage to India*. The books, in their undisturbed, airless ranks, were arranged according to size; there were no unseemly gaps, no volume slumped against another.

He heard Mrs Lavington say, 'Mind you put things back in the right places.'

He took out *The Seven Pillars of Wisdom*, sat down on the arm of a leather chair and began to read. He became aware that the room was falling silent around him. He felt Charlotte standing over him; 'Nick! You can't just sit there *reading* the books!'

He looked up. 'Why not? It's about time someone did.'

She flung a glance towards the old woman. 'Nick . . . Honestly!'

Mrs Lavington said, 'What did he say?'

Nick closed *The Seven Pillars* and returned it to the shelf. 'I said it's high time someone read these books. But I don't think it's going to be me. Thanks for the lunch – it was very good. Lots of it, too.'

He walked out of the room. None of them spoke. He caught, for an instant, the old woman's stare, stupid with disbelief; he could feel all those other incredulous eyes upon him, coffee cups halted half-way to lips, cigar smoke trembling in shafts of sunlight. It was as though he had snapped his fingers 57 and frozen them all to a tableau. He knew at once what it made him think of and as he went out through the front door he said it aloud, and began to laugh: 'You're nothing but a pack of cards!'

He walked across the gravel and into the drive. He heard Charlotte shouting something. He looked back and waved. She was standing at the top of the flight of steps, as bright and glossy as some handsome animal, an antelope, perhaps, and she aroused, he noted with satisfaction, just about as much lust as would an antelope. He waved again and walked on, down the drive, on and on – he didn't recall it being so long – past an open five-barred white gate that said PRIVATE, NO ENTRY and out on to the road. He went along the verge for twenty yards or so and then settled himself comfortably at an angle to the traffic, with his thumb stuck out high into the spring wind.

READ MORE IN PENGUIN

For complete information about books available from Penguin and how to order them, please write to us at the appropriate address below. Please note that for copyright reasons the selection of books varies from country to country.

IN THE UNITED KINGDOM: Please write to *Dept. JC, Penguin Books Ltd, FREEPOST, West Drayton, Middlesex UB7 0BR.*
If you have any difficulty in obtaining a title, please send your order with the correct money, plus ten per cent for postage and packaging, to *PO Box No. 11, West Drayton, Middlesex UB7 0BR.*

IN THE UNITED STATES: Please write to *Consumer Sales, Penguin USA, P.O. Box 999, Dept. 17109, Bergenfield, New Jersey 07621-0120.* VISA and MasterCard holders call 1-800-253-6476 to order all Penguin titles.

IN CANADA: Please write to *Penguin Books Canada Ltd, 10 Alcorn Avenue, Suite 300, Toronto, Ontario M4V 3B2.*

IN AUSTRALIA: Please write to *Penguin Books Australia Ltd, P.O. Box 257, Ringwood, Victoria 3134.*

IN NEW ZEALAND: Please write to *Penguin Books (NZ) Ltd, Private Bag 102902, North Shore Mail Centre, Auckland 10.*

IN INDIA: Please write to *Penguin Books India Pvt Ltd, 706 Eros Apartments, 56 Nehru Place, New Delhi 110 019.*

IN THE NETHERLANDS: Please write to *Penguin Books Netherlands bv, Postbus 3507, NL-1001 AH Amsterdam.*

IN GERMANY: Please write to *Penguin Books Deutschland GmbH, Metzlerstrasse 26, 60594 Frankfurt am Main.*

IN SPAIN: Please write to *Penguin Books S. A., Bravo Murillo 19, 1o B, 28015 Madrid.*

IN ITALY: Please write to *Penguin Italia s.r.l., Via Felice Casati 20, I-20124 Milano.*

IN FRANCE: Please write to *Penguin France S. A., 17 rue Lejeune, F-31000 Toulouse.*

IN JAPAN: Please write to *Penguin Books Japan, Ishikiribashi Building, 2-5-4, Suido, Bunkyo-ku, Tokyo 112.*

IN GREECE: Please write to *Penguin Hellas Ltd, Dimocritou 3, GR-106 71 Athens.*

IN SOUTH AFRICA: Please write to *Longman Penguin Southern Africa (Pty) Ltd, Private Bag X08, Bertsham 2013.*